Crosby,
    May your journey
always lead you to
where you need to be
♡ Brendon, Rae,
    & Rylynn

Dedicated to Kristyn, Ana, Wade,
and Patricia, the eternal butterfly chaser. —ZM

Library of Congress Cataloging-in-Publication Data available.

ISBN 978-1-7972-1010-0

Manufactured in China.

Design by Sara Gillingham Studio.
Handlettering by Zach Manbeck.
Typeset in Brandon Grotesque and Director's Cut Pro.
The illustrations in this book were rendered in gouache and various mixed media, then edited digitally.

10 9 8 7 6 5 4 3 2 1

Chronicle books and gifts are available at special quantity discounts to corporations,
professional associations, literacy programs,
and other organizations. For details and discount information,
please contact our premiums department at corporatesales@chroniclebooks.com or at 1-800-759-0190.

Chronicle Books LLC
680 Second Street
San Francisco, California 94107

Chronicle Books—we see things differently. Become part of our community at www.chroniclekids.com.

YOU

ARE

HERE

Zach Manbeck

chronicle books·san francisco

YOU are here.

And from here,

you can go anywhere!

But how will you find your way?

BEGIN!

Everyone begins differently.
So whether you walk, skip,
dance, or sit . . .

be your own
kind of brave.

EXPLORE

Wander in every direction!

TAKE
YOUR
TIME

Some will be
far ahead of you.

Others will be
miles behind you.

Be thankful for who's
right beside you.

FALL DOWN!

Slip, trip, and scrape
your knees, and then . . .

LOOK

with curious eyes.

SEE

with an
adventurous
heart.

BE
PATIENT

You'll find your way . . .

if you let it find you.

Remember,

you're on your way . . .

in your own way!

And TODAY

Exactly where you are meant to be.